To Pio, who almost never laughs when I fall,
and to Mallory Loehr, my favorite dancing queen—S.C.
For Sabrina—P.P.

Text copyright © 2002 by Shana Corey
Illustrations copyright © 2002 by Pamela Paparone
All rights reserved under International and Pan-American Copyright Conventions.
Published in the United States by Random House, Inc., New York, and simultaneously in
Canada by Random House of Canada Limited, Toronto.
RANDOM HOUSE and colophon are registered trademarks of Random House, Inc.

www.randomhouse.com/kids

Library of Congress Cataloging-in-Publication Data:
Corey, Shana.
Ballerina bear / by Shana Corey ; illustrated by Pamela Paparone.
p. cm.
Summary: Two bears with very different talents perform together at the ballet school recital.
ISBN 0-375-81416-7 (trade) — ISBN 0-375-91416-1 (lib. bdg.)
[1. Ballet dancing—Fiction. 2. Bears—Fiction.] I. Paparone, Pamela, ill. II. Title.
PZ7.C8155 Bal 2002
[E]—dc21
2001048381
Printed in Hong Kong   First Edition August 2002   10 9 8 7 6 5 4 3 2 1

Ballerina Bear

By Shana Corey

Costume and Set Design by
Pamela Paparone

starring
Bernice

special guest appearance by
Bertram

Bernice loved to dance.

She loved to cha-cha.

She loved to cancan.

She loved to clog.

She loved to tap-dance

and tango

and two-step.
But most of all . . .

. . . Bernice loved ballet!

Every Wednesday and Saturday,
Bernice went to ballet class.

There was only one little problem.

Whenever she twirled, she tumbled.

Whenever she leaped, she landed in a lump.

And whenever she stood on her tiptoes . . .

. . . she tripped and her tutu ripped!
In short, Bernice was *not* graceful.

"You will *never* be a ballerina,
Bernice," everyone said.
Bernice was heartbroken.

But she kept taking lessons and

practicing,

practicing,

practicing.

"You look beautiful,"
Bernice's mommy said.

"I know," said Bernice sadly.
"But beauty isn't everything."

Then one day in
ballet class, there was
a new dancer.
His name was Bertram.
Bertram was the best ballet
dancer in the whole school.
He never fell, or tumbled,
or tripped.
He was perfect.
There was only one
little problem.

Whenever Bertram danced, people fell asleep.
They tried not to, but they couldn't help it.

In short, Bertram was *boring*.

By the time he did his last perfect pirouette,
everyone was snoring.

Everyone except Bernice.

"Be my partner," begged Bernice.

"Okay," said Bertram.

The very next day, Bernice and Bertram bought matching ballet costumes.

They practiced every day for a month. Soon it was time for the annual ballet-school recital.

Bertram came out on stage
and did a perfect plié.
People began to yawn.

Then Bernice came out
and pliéd . . . *plop!*
People opened their eyes.

Bertram leaped.
Bernice lumped.

Bertram twirled.
Bernice tumbled.

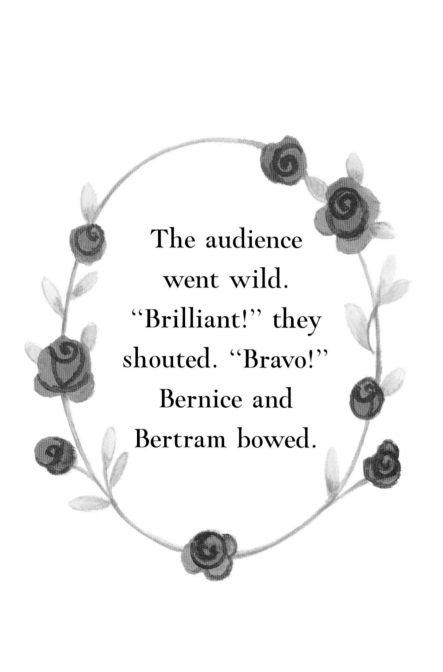

The audience
went wild.
"Brilliant!" they
shouted. "Bravo!"
Bernice and
Bertram bowed.

"Bertram," said Bernice, "you are not boring at all."
"Bernice," said Bertram, "you are a wonderful ballerina."

"Thank you," said Bernice. "I always *knew* I would be."